Dipa Ruwala lives in Greater London. She is a part-time lawyer, part-time writer, full-time wife to her fellow lawyer husband and mum to her two children. This is her first children's book which she hopes will inspire children and make them smile.

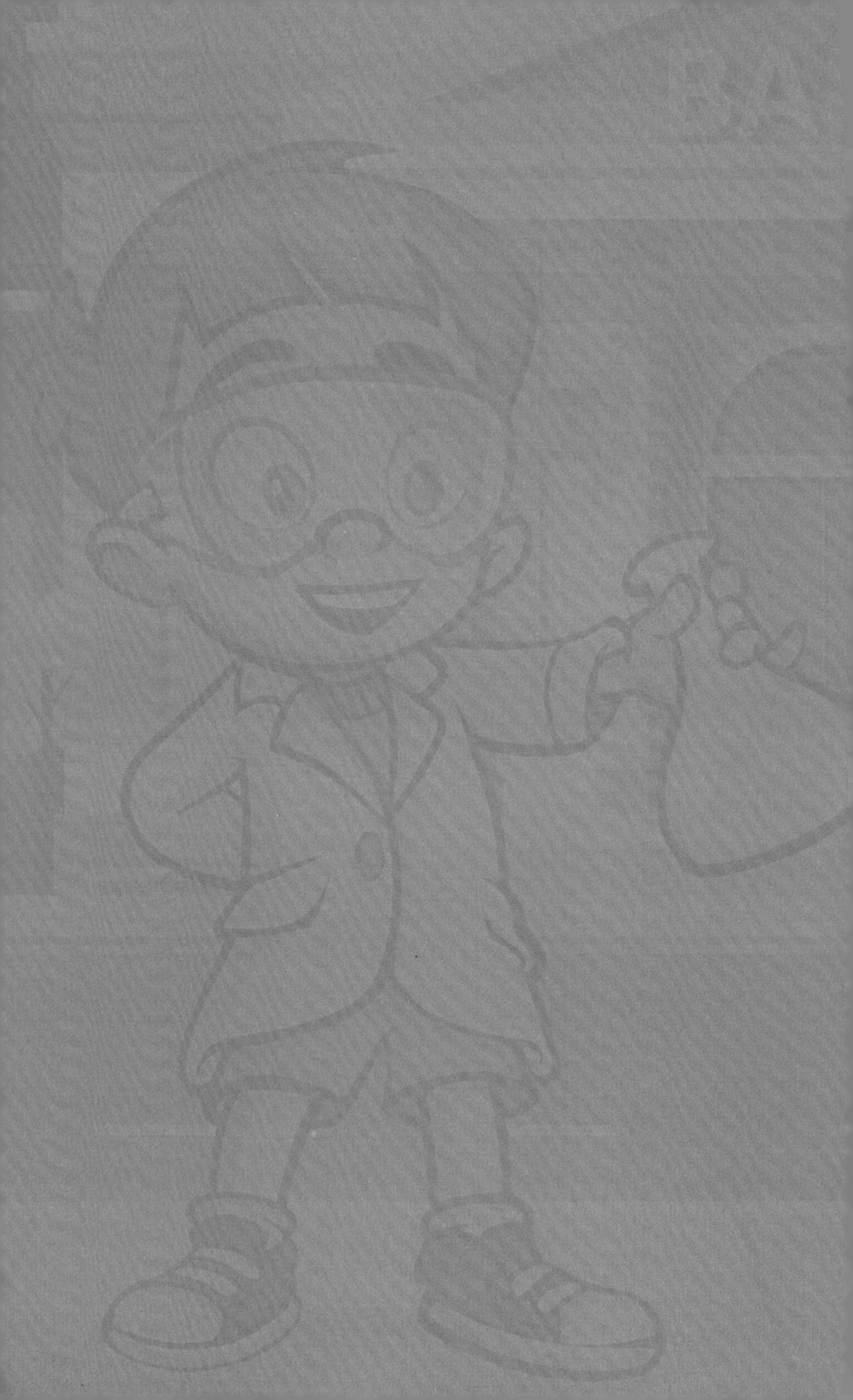

HUGO BAXTER AND THE GREAT BANK ROBBERY

BANK

Dipa Ruwala

AUSTIN MACAULEY PUBLISHERS™
LONDON • CAMBRIDGE • NEW YORK • SHARJAH

A CIP catalogue record for this title is available from the British Library.

ISBN 9781528993319 (Paperback)
ISBN 9781528993326 (ePub e-book)

www.austinmacauley.com

First Published 2022
Austin Macauley Publishers Ltd®
1 Canada Square
Canary Wharf
London
E14 5AA

To, Maya and Jayen, always.

Author's note

Always do what you enjoy, even if it makes you different from others. Don't feel you have to follow the crowd. It is your differences that make you special and unique. If you stay true to yourself and do what you love you will always succeed in life.

CHAPTER 1

Hello, I'm Hugo Baxter. I'm nine years old, or so I've been told, but I don't believe them. I'm pretty certain they have made an error on this one, which is perfectly plausible, given that human beings are prone to making errors. Given my knowledge and independence, I'm more likely to be a rather small 34-year-old (I think I was adopted). However, I have decided to humour them and play along. 'Them' being my parents, of course, and playing along meaning blowing out the number of candles they decide to put on my birthday cake, smiling when I am referred to as nine and worst of all sitting in a year 4 class with other nine-year-olds. I would much rather be sitting in a classroom full of adults. So much more fun and interesting. If I have to sit through another conversation about the teenage mutant ninja turtles, I think I may spontaneously combust!

At school, the boys my age are divided into two groups. Two very closed groups, I might add. The first group is the footballer group. They spend every second of every minute of every playtime chasing after a ball as if their life depended on it. I really don't understand it, do you? The second group talk of nothing other than computer games. I can't even tell you the names of them, I just hear these discussions from a distance because, as I mentioned earlier, these groups are very closed. There must be some form of initiation to get in, a quiz on computer games or the demonstration of a very rare football skill. Anyway, I spend every second of every minute of every playtime devising my next science experiment. Christopher Simms, who likes neither football or computer games, sits with me and calls himself my assistant. I actually don't think he is particularly passionate about science, but he is nice enough, friendly and takes notes when I am thinking up ideas. It's quite nice actually, having a friend.

I live with my parents and very annoying older sister, Izzy (who is obsessed with someone called Justin Bieber, maybe an environmentalist or a human rights campaigner), on the outskirts of London. The huge advantage of this is that it is not far to the science museum in London. Have you been? If not, you really should go. It's amazing. You see I love the science museum because I love all things scientific. The thing about science is that it is logical, helps to make sense of the world and by using scientific techniques we can make the world a better place. That is my ambition. To make the world a better place using science. I think of Albert Einstein, Alexander Graham Bell, Thomas Edison, Marie Curie and Stephen Hawking. The greats! I have turned my bedroom into a scientific laboratory and I am already testing certain theories I have with respect to renewable energy and the reduction of pollution. There is only one slightly major hindrance to my work.

"Hugo, clean this mess up at once!" screams Mum as she recoils at the smell of burning sulphur and the sight of a blue liquid spillage all over the cream carpet. Whose idea was it to put cream carpet in my bedroom anyway? Okay, so that was an experiment that went slightly wrong, but according to this book

I have about the growth mindset, it is important to get things wrong and to learn from your mistakes. So, I am never worried about failed experiments. However, what does concern me is my parents' failure to understand that I want to change the world and that my bedroom is my science laboratory and that I can't keep cleaning it away! My parents always seem stressed, which is understandable really. You see, they are both teachers. That really explains everything, don't you think? My dad teaches history and my mum French at a secondary school. Their lack of knowledge in science really doesn't help me.

"Mum, it's not a mess, it's my experiment," I reply hoping that she will relent.

"Hugo, this is not the place for experiments," Mum replies curtly.

"Tidy up and downstairs for dinner in ten minutes." She turns to leave looking exasperated.

Reluctantly, I clear away and wipe up the spillage, leaving a rather large blue stain on the carpet. I need to do something, I think, to show them what an amazing scientist I am and what I can achieve. I mull over this thought on my way down to dinner, my sister, Izzy, pushing me out of the way on her way down. I'm sure I will think of something.

CHAPTER 2

The doorbell rings and it's Christopher. He rings the doorbell at precisely 8.20 am every school morning. He lives 12 doors away and always stops off to 'collect' us on his way. I say us as Izzy has to walk us to school on her way to her school which is five minutes further up the road. Our parents leave at 7 am so Izzy is in charge of breakfast and getting me to school on time. I feel mildly offended by the notion that they think I'm incapable of this, but then they do think I'm nine. What they don't know is that Izzy leaves me completely to my own devices and spends over an hour in the bathroom painting her face. I think she calls it make up. If only they knew.

"Hi Hugo, are you ready?" He looks especially keen today.

"Hello Christopher, yes just waiting for Izzy," I respond.

"How did the sulphur experiment go last night?"

"Well, not as I had planned," I didn't want to mention Mum's obsession about tidiness and having to clear everything away before I really had a chance to examine things.

"But I'm going to give it another go."

"Great, maybe I can come over to help this evening," he says optimistically.

That's it, I think. If Christopher is around, Mum will pretty much let us get on with things. Everyone knows parents are much more diplomatic when friends are over.

"That would be great," I reply with a smile.

Izzy comes running down the stairs, her face looking entirely different to what it had done earlier this morning. How can paint make such a difference? She looks like a different person. Hmm... I wonder what this 'make up' contains? The beginning of a new experiment forming in my mind is sharply interrupted.

"Come on you two, we're late!" Izzy shouts as she runs out of the door. Christopher races after her whilst simultaneously looking through his national geographic animal cards. I linger looking around. You see observation is a very important part of science.

"Hugo, hurry up!" Izzy screams and I pick up my speed.

We live at 96 Newport Street. As we walk up the garden path, we turn left towards the shops and school. After our house there are three more houses then shops, a road to cross and then our school, New Cross Primary School. I have prepared a very detailed map which I have included here for your reference.

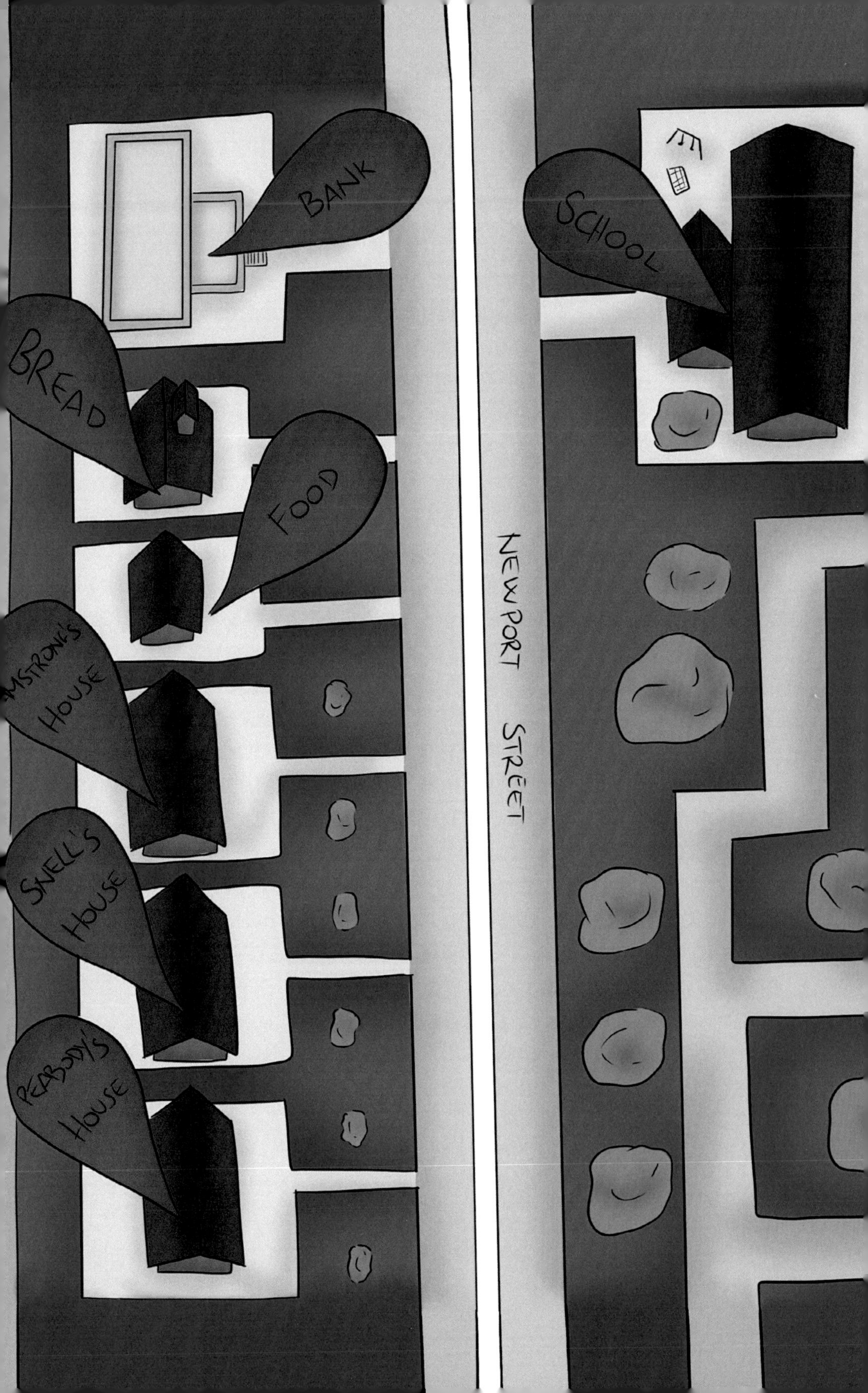
BANK
BREAD
FOOD
MSTRONG'S HOUSE
SNELL'S HOUSE
PEABODY'S HOUSE
SCHOOL
NEWPORT STREET

Although a running commentary of my route to school sounds a little dull, it is actually much more interesting than it sounds!

Next door to us, in number 98, live Mr and Mrs Peabody. I asked them once how old they were (Mum told me off for being rude, which confused me as it is a very matter-of-fact question) and discovered that Mr Peabody is in fact 85 and Mrs Peabody 83. This surprised me as they both look very good for their age and don't even need walking sticks. They are, actually, very friendly and always come out to wave to us as we walk to school. I once overheard Mum saying that she was worried about Mrs Peabody's knees. I can't see why, they looked perfectly normal to me? They didn't seem to get out much, however ironically were always wearing coats and hats when they came to the door. Very curious. (It is important to have a curious mind if you want to be a scientist.) Mrs Peabody always smelt of a combination of Wave and Vax and mints. (Wave and Vax was apparently very popular in the 1980s. You sprinkle a white powder onto your carpet and then hoover over it. It is supposed to make your carpet smell very fresh.) They have a son who lives in Australia. I remember Mum saying to them once that they should go out and visit him and get some sunshine and them saying they would love to but that it was very expensive to fly to Australia. Well, I suppose it is on the other side of the world.

Next door to Mr and Mrs Peabody lives Mr Snell. I actually think his name was once Mr Smell, but he was so embarrassed that he changed it to Snell instead. Perfectly understandable, and would explain why he is always sucking on a mint. I haven't actually asked him how old he is, but I suspect he is around 45 as he looks a similar age to my dad. There is a reason why I haven't actually asked him his age. I would describe him as a most unapproachable man. He never comes out to wave at us as we walk past (Mr and Mrs Peabody have set high standards) and we often see him peeking from behind the curtains. Looks very suspicious if you ask me. And when we do see him, he makes a face (which I think is supposed to be a smile although he is clearly not good at smiling as it doesn't look like a smile. I wonder if he could attend smiling lessons) and doesn't say anything. Just sticks his nose further in the air and walks past. He always wears the same green coat, even in summer! I have seen him wear that coat for as long as I can remember, and if my calculations are correct, that would be 34 years!

As we reach the house next door to Mr Snell, number 102, the Armstrong family come out. If there was ever a name that described a family well, it was this one. The Armstrong family are tall. When I say tall, I am not referring to them being taller than the average height person, I mean lamp post tall! They could barely fit through the entrance to their front door. Mr and Mrs Armstrong are so tall that they really did have to bend over to get into the front door (must be very annoying). Their son, Audi, (yes, you've guessed it, he was named after the car) is in my class, and his head hits the door frame as he comes in and out of the house. Their daughter, Candy, who I think is five can just about get through the door with an inch to spare. They really do need to invest in a bigger and taller doorway. So, going back to Audi, he is in my class and if you are wondering, is in the 'football group'. In fact, he is the leader and really doesn't seem to like anyone who doesn't like football. I wouldn't say he is a bully, but it seems that anyone who doesn't like football or play football is invisible. That would explain the number of times he has walked straight into me, I'm clearly invisible to him. I have heard of selective hearing, but could there also be something called selective sight…hmmm, I wonder. The Armstrongs push straight past us and head on to school.

Between number 102 and school there are two shops and a bank. The first is a grocery shop owned by Mr Thomas, a nice man who always seems to smell of broccoli. He must eat buckets of it, which would explain his healthy complexion given that broccoli is full of anti-oxidants.

Next door to the grocers is a bakery owned by Mr and Mrs Patel. The Patels used to own a news agents. However, one Christmas they received a voucher for a bakery course from their son and they loved it so much they decided that's all they wanted to do. So, they turned their news agents into a bakery and I must admit they are actually really good.

Next to the bakery is Bluebird Bank. Everyone in the area uses the bank and by 1 pm the queues are normally out onto the street with people trying to do their banking before they close for lunch at 1.30 pm. Our school is on the other side of the road opposite the bank. (Please refer to the map above.)

"Come on, Hugo!" shouts Christopher.

"The bell is about to go."

We race through the gates as Izzy shouts goodbye and heads on to her school. I hope you enjoyed the commentary.

CHAPTER 3

In terms of my school, it really is in need of some modernisation. Our headteacher, Mr Bucket, is very proud of the school's history, having been a place of refuge for many families during the Second World War and seems to want to preserve it as it was in 1939. That's fine of course, history is great, although not really my subject. My only slight issue is from a safety perspective. I mean, putting aesthetics aside (peeling paint, cracked windows, ceiling plaster giving off sprinkles of white dust at regular intervals and please don't get me started on the toilets), the building does look set to crumble. All families have been assured that there is no immediate danger to the children (the word 'immediate' did concern me slightly but everyone else seemed fine with this), however there was no mention of a structural engineer having undertaken a site visit. On my inspection there seemed to be evidence of subsidence and material instability. On the next page is a drawing of the corridor outside my classroom. What do you think?

I walk into class 4L. The classroom door is hanging on its one bottom hinge and therefore it sits at an angle and we all have to try to squeeze past in single file.

"Make sure you don't touch the door as you come in, we don't want it to fall onto anyone," Miss Little sings. I say sings as she is incapable of shouting and when she wants to be heard over 30 children

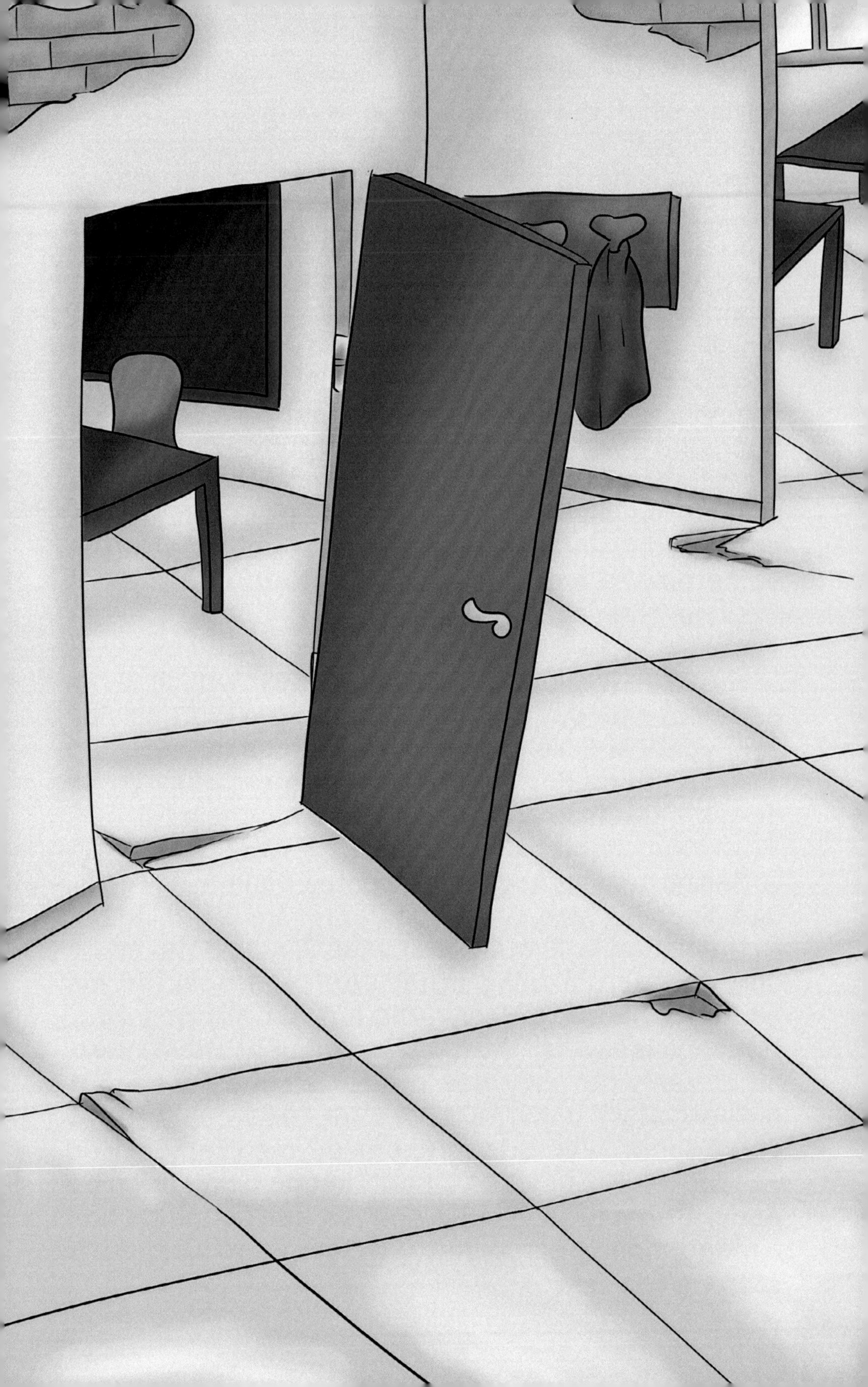

talking all at the same time, she sings.

Miss Little is our teacher. She is quite nice I suppose. However, she is one of those teachers who is positive towards each and every child, even when they haven't done their work or have misbehaved. I understand the theory behind this; however I am all for consequences if a child doesn't do what they are supposed to. The other thing that is quite annoying is that she spends the last half an hour of each and every day playing her guitar and having a sing-song (as I explained earlier, she really likes singing) which I suppose is fine if you are five, but wouldn't that time be better spent teaching us something? I would much rather hear about Louis Pasteur than sing a song.

My desk is closest to the window, which I am especially pleased about. When I am waiting for everyone to finish their work, I stare outside and think of ideas for my next experiment. Miss Little doesn't seem to notice, which is very helpful.

Behind me sits Audi Armstrong. I don't mind really, and given his size, it's much better he is behind me rather than in front otherwise I would never be able to see anything other than the back of his head, which quite frankly is not that interesting. My only issue is that, as previously mentioned, he doesn't actually see me (given that I am not a footballer) and therefore he talks over me to Jay Kapoor who sits in front of me (very skilled footballer from what I hear, hence being seen by Audi). I say talks, but he sounds as though he has a megaphone permanently attached to his mouth.

It's very annoying when you're in deep thought about the periodic table and you are interrupted by Audi bellowing something that doesn't even fall into the definition of a sentence.

"Oi Jay, Sat result, what ey?" I'm not sure what this even means?!

Jay turns around and looks over me.

"Oh yeah crazy, huh?" Jay responds as if he has completely understood what Audi has said.

"Yeah innit." It's almost as if I'm watching an informative documentary of how language was first used in the stone age to communicate primary needs.

Both smile and put their heads down and carry on with their reading. I still can't understand what the discussion was about but at least they seem satisfied.

We are reading the book Mr Cat. I wouldn't exactly put it into the category of acclaimed English literature but everyone else seems to enjoy it. It's about a cat who has a secret life that he lives, when the family he lives with are out of the house. I suppose in a way I can relate to this. On the outside I am a nine-year-old boy who goes to school and enjoys science. On the inside I am a 34-year-old scientist trying to change the world.

"So, who can name some of Mr Cat's characteristics?" Miss Little squeaks. When she is not singing, she is squeaking.

"He's a cat!" shouts out Audi.

"Well done, Audi," sings Miss Little.

"He has whiskers!" shouts out Jay.

"That's great," beams Miss Little.

"He has paws!" shouts out Luke (he's in the computer game crowd).

"Such wonderful answers," Miss Little sings again.

I consider shouting out that I think Mr Cat is living a paradoxical existence and feels his intellect is undervalued by the family that cares for him and is therefore searching for some way of expressing this intellect. However, I decide not to. Instead I stare out into the playground looking for some inspiration. Surely, there must be something I can do to prove to my parents that I am a great scientist.

CHAPTER 4

After a really long and tedious maths lesson reciting the four times table, which having reviewed the national curriculum online I'm sure we were supposed to have covered in year 2, and another 30 minute sing song, the bell rings. "Don't forget, your projects on Australia are due after half term," sings Miss Little.

One week's half-term. How many experiments can I get done in one week? I stand up to collect my things only to be knocked over by Audi, who doesn't even notice me at his feet.

"Kick about?" booms Audi over me while I try to scramble to my feet, trying to position myself in a way that Audi does not step on me.

"Ugh!" grunts Jay. I think that may have been a yes?

I gather my things and make for the door slightly more dishevelled than when I entered it that morning.

"Hugo, I thought I could come back to your house now and call my mum from there." Christopher was beaming. I had forgotten about the plan for him to come over and help me with the sulphur experiment. Despite us being friends since nursery, he has only ever been to my house twice before (obviously not including the daily 8.20 am call at the front door) and that would explain his slightly excitable energy which manifested itself in him bouncing about from one foot to the other whilst still trying to walk.

"That's fine, Christopher," I reply as I look beyond the school gates and notice a lot of commotion which was very unusual for our road.

"I wonder what's happening out there." I point at the large crowd that had gathered across the street from our school.

"Probably a sale on in Mr Patel's bakery, I hope it's the apple turnovers, they are my favourites!" Christopher replies, his excitable energy growing to the point that he is now almost skipping. He actually looks like he needs to go to the toilet!

We cross the street and notice police outside Bluebird Bank. The bank is cordoned off with yellow police tape and is clearly a crime scene. I see Mr Snell and Mrs Armstrong looking completely shocked and Mr and Mrs Peabody. Mr and Mrs Peabody are actually outside of their house! I don't believe it! They don't look very well.

"Are you okay, Mrs Peabody? What's happened?" I ask her.

"Haven't you heard; someone has robbed Bluebird Bank. Taken everything whilst the cashiers were having their lunch. All our money is gone." Mrs Peabody puts a tissue to her face which is slightly odd as there are no tears and definitely no runny nose!

"Do they know who it was?" I question slightly concerned. I'm sure I heard Mum and Dad talking about putting all their savings into Bluebird Bank.

Mrs Peabody looks right at me, "No, whoever did this, left no trace at all. Managed to turn the CCTV off too." She puts the tissue to her face again. Mr Peabody says nothing, just stares right ahead. They must both be very upset. They didn't have that much money to begin with and now they have lost everything. I look down at Mrs Peabody's knees. They still look okay to me.

"Go home, Hugo, this is no place for children, your parents wouldn't want you standing around here." Mr Patel looks at me and hands me a bag containing two apple turnovers. Christopher looks in the bag and immediately the thought of the bank having been emptied of all our money leaves him and he grabs one and starts eating. Oh, how nice it is to be young and innocent.

"Thanks Mr Patel," I say.

"Yes, thanks Mr Patel," Christopher says as flakes of pastry spray out all over his uniform.

When we arrive home, Mum and Dad are already there. They are looking even more anxious than they normally do. As I walk through to the kitchen, I notice a police officer writing some notes and as he looks up at us, he smiles.

"Just asking around to find out if anybody saw what happened at the Bluebird Bank."

"Unfortunately, we were both at work and only rushed home when we received a call from Mr Patel about the robbery. We really do need to find out who did this as all our savings were in the Bluebird Bank, and we were hoping to take the children on holiday this summer."

"I understand, however, so far we have found no forensic evidence that can lead us to catching anyone." The policeman shakes his head.

Hmmm…I think. Forensic evidence. I run upstairs and pull open my wardrobe door and reach up to the top shelf. That's it, I've got it! My forensic science kit. I knew this would prove to be useful one day. There has to be some evidence I can find. I will get back Mum and Dad's money and show them what a great scientist I can be!

CHAPTER 5

Day 1 of Investigation. Saturday

So, what do you think? Do you think I can do this? I'm pretty certain I can. It's 8 am on Saturday morning and I'm ready to go. The plan? To go to Bluebird Bank and find some evidence. I have my forensic kit packed, determined and ready to go (well, once I have spoken to Mum and Dad and they are happy for me to go). This may cause a slight problem, you see, since yesterday Mum and Dad are extremely worried that there are robbers running around outside. I have never seen Dad lock all the windows and doors in the whole house and then recheck them. He even locked the windows in the attic. I mean, how is anyone even going to get up there?

In the kitchen, Mum and Dad are at the table looking as though they have lost all their money in the world, which is a very accurate description because actually they have.

"Mum, Dad, I'm just going to pop out for a little walk," I say trying to sound cheerful.

A look of complete and utter alarm spreads across Mum's face. "What do you mean a walk? It's 8 o'clock in the morning, and you know it's not safe out there, not with the robbers on the loose. It's caused total panic in the area."

"Mum, I'm just going to pop to Mr Patel's bakery and then maybe over to the library. I will be back for lunch."

Mum is weary from worry and she gives in.

"Okay," she says, "but I want you to be home by 1 pm." I'm already running out of the door. No time to lose and lots to do.

I look around to see if I can spot any unusual behaviour. Newport Street is empty. Everyone must be feeling like Mum. Scared. However, although I understand this, it must be the worst time to stay at home. Vital clues could be missed. I turn left out of our gate and pass Mr and Mrs Peabody. They don't come to the door today, probably afraid like Mum. Their curtains are still drawn, which is unusual. I hope they are okay. Mr Snell's house looks the same as always, no change there and the Armstrong family must still be asleep as there seems to be no sign of anyone. Mr Thomas's grocery shop and Mr Patel's bakery are open as usual, but with no customers. Everyone is staying away. Bluebird Bank is still cordoned off, however there is no one there and the door to the bank is open. I walk in to find Mrs Willis, the cleaner. She lives at the other end of Newport Street. Cleaning is not a good thing when I am trying to find clues!

"Oh, hello there, Hugo, what are you doing here?"

"I was wondering if I could have a look around. I'm, um, really interested in forensic science and thought I could look around here."

"Well, I'm not supposed to allow anyone in, after all it is a crime scene, but what harm could a nine-years-old boy do, eh?"

"Thanks, Mrs Willis," I reply as politely as I can. I am ever so grateful to her for allowing me in.

"Mind you, I'll be leaving in an hour, so I will have to lock up then."

"That's fine. Um, Mrs Willis have you done the hoovering yet?" I ask.

The carpet looks spotless, and I know that if Mrs Willis has hoovered, my chances of finding anything useful are very limited.

"Oh no, the carpet seems to have been hoovered already, quite curious really, it was a mess yesterday morning and I thought I would do it today but it's already been done. It must have been the police?" She looks utterly confused and to be quite frank so am I. Why would the police hoover the carpet?

I walk around the bank and not one thing looks out of place. Even if something had been left by the robbers, it is well and truly gone now. Hopefully, the police forensics have found something which would be great for everyone getting their money back, but maybe not so great in showing Mum and Dad what a great scientist I am. I take out my magnifying glass and scan the floor. In between the carpet fibres, I notice some white specks that look a little like flour, or icing sugar. I wonder what this could be? I put on some gloves and pull out some loose carpet fibres with a pair of tweezers and place them into one of my crime scene bags and as I bend down, I smell something very familiar, but can't quite put my finger on what it is.

I walk out to the front of the bank again. How could anyone have got into the bank without anyone noticing? Mum and Dad said the robbery happened at 1.30 pm. This is a busy time of the day. How can no one have noticed? I walk round to the side of the bank and notice a wrapper on the floor. I pick it up. It's a mint wrapper. Drawing below. It could be significant, or alternatively it could just be a random wrapper thrown onto the floor by someone who is not interested in looking after the environment.

I go back inside and start sketching a plan of the bank and where staff would have been at the time of the robbery. They were all sitting behind the glass wall eating their lunch (apparently, Cheese and Tomato toasties from Mr Patel's bakery).

Any ideas of how someone could have got in and got to the safe without the staff noticing?

As I'm leaving, a thought occurs to me.

"Mrs Willis, is there any other way of getting into and out of the bank?"

"Yes, Hugo, the back door. It's through the store room. It leads out onto a brick patio, which runs along the back of all the houses on this side of Newport Street. Come on, let me show you."

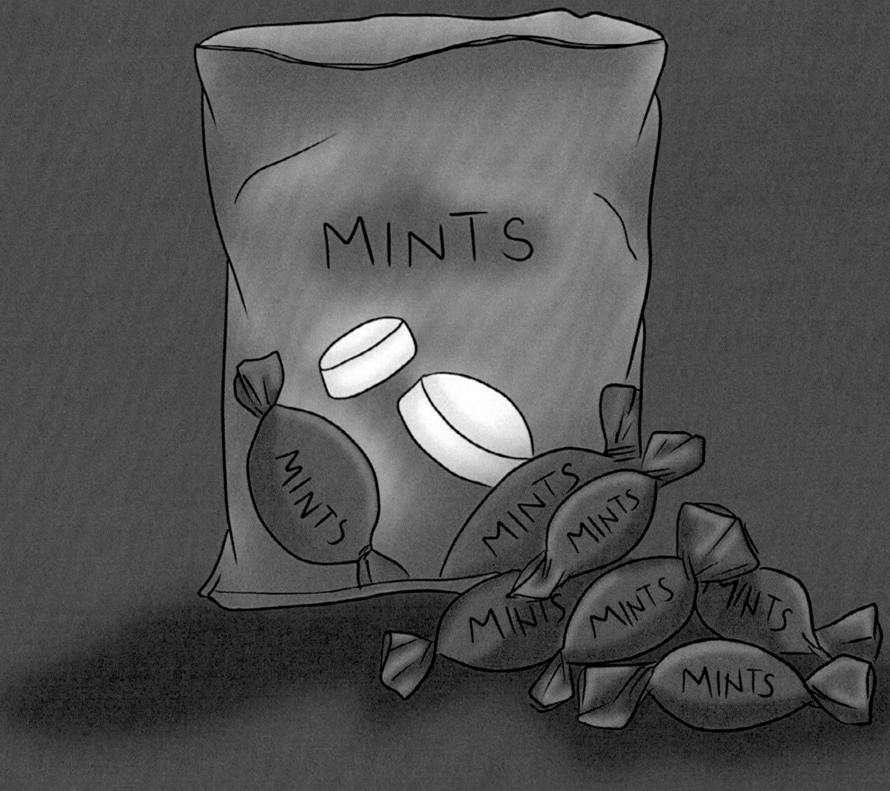
MINTS
MINTS
MINTS
MINTS
MINTS
MINTS
MINTS

Mrs Willis opens the store cupboard door and there on the back wall is the door that leads to the back of the bank. She opens it and goes outside. I manage to climb up onto the brick wall and look to the left. I see the back of Mr Patel's shop, Mr Thomas's grocery shop, the back of the Armstrong house, Mr Snell's house, Mr and Mrs Peabody's house and even the back of our house. Mum is hanging out the washing. I really wish she wouldn't hang my pants up in the garden. So embarrassing. I wouldn't mind if they were the periodic table ones, but the space alien ones Mum bought me really are a step too far.

There are no walls or fences between the bank and the two shops. The first fence is the Armstrong fence. It doesn't look very stable. I may need to let Mrs Armstrong know. It could be a safety hazard.

I use my fingerprint dust, but find no evidence of fingerprints on the inside or outside of the back door.

"Do the bank staff always keep this door locked?" I ask Mrs Willis.

"Yes, they do, however I heard from Mrs Smith who heard from Mrs Ball who heard from Mrs Curran that Mrs Frank, who has the keys, forgot to lock the back door before lunch. Apparently, a stray cat was meowing at the back door for some time, so she unlocked the door to put some milk out for the cat and was in such a rush to get back to lunch so that her toastie wouldn't get cold that she forgot to lock the door." Mrs Willis looks out of breath after that. I don't mention to her that actually cats are lactose intolerant, and that Mrs Frank shouldn't have put any milk out for the cat, but it seems irrelevant in the circumstances.

As we head back inside, I notice a white box attached to the brick wall at the back of the bank. Its flap door is slightly ajar.

"What's that, Mrs Willis?" I ask.

"Oh, that's the electrical box, it contains all the bank's electrical cables, not sure why it's open though?" she says trying to shut the door.

"Thanks, Mrs Willis." That was all very helpful.

On the way back home, I notice a sign stuck to a tree.

Hmmm....I think. A missing cat.

CHAPTER 6

Day 2 of Investigation. Sunday

I have told Mum that I am going to Christopher's house, which is sort of true as I am going to drop off his bag that he left at my house on Friday. Mum looked pleased as I think she worries about me not having enough friends. She really needn't worry, I really am quite content, but I suppose it is part of the job description of a parent to worry. She is still very worried about the robbers and says that I must not talk to any strangers.

Before going to Christopher's, I am going to number 22. Technically, speaking to the person at number 22 is equivalent to talking to a stranger as I don't actually know who lives there, but I'm sure it's not a robber (I don't think a robber would be leaving posters with their address and telephone number on lamp posts) so I think I will be okay. I need to find out more about this missing cat.

The door is answered by an elderly man holding, very unexpectedly, a cat!

"Hello, my name is Hugo and I noticed your sign about a missing cat and wondered whether you had found it, but I see you have."

"Oh, yes." He smiles, "Casper went missing over a week ago which is very strange as he has never so much as left the garden, and then he reappeared last night in the front garden, it was very strange. He looks like he was well fed, however has had a bit of an upset stomach. Probably eaten something that didn't agree with him. Also smells very fresh. I think someone gave him a bath. But thank you for calling, very kind." He smiles.

"I'm glad you have found him."

I turn to walk away. Hmm...an upset stomach, I wonder if that was caused by milk? Fresh smell? I wonder what that could be?

Dropping the bag to Christopher became more problematic than I had initially thought.

"Hugo, stay for lunch, let's do another experiment." I thought back to the second failed attempt on Friday evening of burning sulphur, which ended up burning a hole the size of an orange through my cream carpet. I now have a hole and a blue stain. Mum is not happy.

"Sorry Christopher, I need to get back, but maybe another day."

"What do you need to get back for? Maybe I can help you."

"Hi, Hugo," Christopher's mum comes to the door smiling. "Come in and stay for lunch."

"Thank you, Mrs Simms, but I really do need to get home to help my parents with a few things, but maybe another day." I back away hoping that the greater the distance between us the less likely it was that I would end up going in.

"How nice. Yes, Hugo, definitely, I will call your mum to arrange something." She waves.

I smile and walk away trying not to think of how Mum will react when she finds out I was not at Christopher's house for very long. Next on my list is telling Mrs Armstrong about her fence. Although, I am in the middle of a huge project as any great scientist will tell you, health and safety comes first.

As I clunk the knocker down on the door of number 102, dust from cracked concrete above me on the porch sprinkles over me like icing sugar being sprinkled on a cake. Mrs Armstrong answers the door bending down significantly to see who I am.

"Oh, hello, Hugo, have you been baking? How lovely."

I dust off the concrete sprinkles. "Um, Mrs Armstrong, I noticed that your back fence looks a little unsteady."

"Sorry, did you say something?"

Was I really that far away from her that she couldn't hear a word that I was saying? I stand on tiptoes and shout as loud as I can.

"Mrs Armstrong, your back fence looks like it may fall down!"

"Oh yes, very strange. It's brand new, only had it put in on Wednesday. It was very strong, and then when I came home from work on Friday afternoon, it was almost falling down. It must be faulty, either that or something very big and heavy has tried to climb it." She chuckles. Very curious.

"Did you say you were working on Friday?!" I ask as loudly as possible.

"Yes Hugo, I was working a shift at the hospital between 10am - 2pm and noticed the fence when I got home."

"Do you think I could take a look?!" I shout again.

"Oh yes, be my guest," she bellows and takes me through to the back garden.

It looks even worse from this side and doesn't look at all like a brand-new fence. I wander towards it and notice what looks like scratch marks. The Armstrongs don't have a pet. I put on my gloves and pull out my fingerprint powder and begin dusting. There are lots of fingerprints on this fence. That would make sense though, wouldn't it? Mr and Mrs Armstrong, Candy, Audi and even the people who delivered the fence. Even so I use my sticky tape to lift off the fingerprints to analyse under my microscope when I get home. I seem to have several different sets of fingerprints. I need to eliminate the Armstrong family fingerprints so that I can focus on the others. Maybe someone jumped over the Armstrong fence. Maybe that's how they got to the bank. Could it have been Mr or Mrs Armstrong?

I go back inside. Mrs Armstrong is cooking a meal in the largest cooking pot I have ever seen. Given their size, this family must get through a lot of food. I notice a TV remote control on the sofa arm in the lounge. Without Mrs Armstrong noticing, I use my fingerprint dust to lift off fingerprints from the remote control. This will help me to eliminate the Armstrongs to see if there are any other fingerprints on the fence. Upstairs I hear Audi and Candy arguing, and the ceiling seems to shake every time they speak. I really don't think these houses were designed for larger than average people. I make a quick exit.

"Thank you, Mrs Armstrong." I call on my way out.
Something or someone definitely climbed the fence. I need to find out who.

CHAPTER 7

Day 3 of the Investigation. Monday

So, the plan today is to try and get as many fingerprints as possible from people on Newport Street. I already have Mr Patels' (recent birthday card) and Mr Thomas' (he popped in for a cup of tea with Mum and Dad yesterday and I have stashed his cup under my bed, can't say I like my room smelling of stale tea, but I can't wash it just yet). The only issue is Mum. She asked me last night if I would like to go to the science museum, and where I would normally jump at the chance, I asked her if we could go towards the end of the week. She immediately rushed over and put her hand over my forehead to check my temperature as parents tend to do. Not very scientific and certainly not an accurate way to tell if a child is unwell, but it seems to make them feel better though. We have now agreed to go on Sunday, that should give me enough time, don't you think?

Right now, to put my plan into action!

"Mum, would it be okay if I popped into Mr and Mrs Peabody's house, I need to find out some facts out about Australia and, as their son lives out there, I thought they may be able to help. I may also ask Mr Snell as I think I heard you mention that he has been to Australia before." Fingers crossed.

"Hugo, I'm not sure, Mr and Mrs Peabody haven't really been themselves since the robbery, they have been quite shaken up by it really. I haven't even seen them come to the door since last week."

"Wouldn't that be a good reason to check up on them Mum? I mean to make sure they are okay." It's working I can tell.

Mum looks at me thoughtfully.

"Well, okay, Hugo, but don't stay long I don't want you to tire them out and the same with Mr Snell. You know he's not keen on visitors."

"Okay, Mum, I won't be long."

I put my forensics kit into my rucksack so as not to draw attention to my investigation and grab a notepad and pen.

Mrs Peabody answers the door looking startled and smelling rather minty. She clearly looks shaken. The robbery must have been a bit of a shock for them. I almost change my mind about taking their fingerprints, but I know I must eliminate them from the investigation. As a scientist, it is important to remain objective and not to let the fact that you like an elderly couple affect your findings. So, I go in.

"What can I do for you, Hugo?" Mrs Peabody asks in a small but cheerful voice. She is hoovering and the familiar smell of Wave and Vax wafts through the house. Hmm…where have I smelt that before?

"I wondered if I could ask you a few questions about Australia. We are learning about it at school, and I thought you may know a little about it as your son lives there."

"Oh, Timothy, yes he has been living in Brisbane for over ten years. Haven't been able to visit him could never afford to, yes come in. Mr Peabody is the best person to ask. I've never been good at facts."

I walk into the spotless living room to find Mr Peabody sitting on the sofa reading Electronic Devices Today. When he sees me, he jumps up putting the magazine face down on the coffee table. I'm not sure why he is embarrassed. I think it's great that he is keeping his mind active!

"Hello, Hugo, how can I help you?"

"Well, I wondered whether you could tell me some facts about Australia as I need to know for a project I am doing for school."

Mr Peabody looks around and I wonder whether he has heard me. I know his hearing is not very good. In the background I can hear Mrs Peabody humming to herself. Is that the Australian national anthem? She must be really missing her son.

After what seems like an unusually long silence he responds, "Oh that's nice. Um, well, myself and Mrs Peabody must go to a doctor's appointment, but you are more than welcome to borrow a book on Australia. Mind you, we will need it back by Friday morning for the nations favourite quiz show in case we need to look up any answers." He hands me a book The Rough Guide to Australia and then calls out to Mrs Peabody.

"Betty, could you please bring a bag for young Hugo here."

Mrs Peabody brings out a bag and puts the book into the bag. Great now I have both their fingerprints. Mrs Peabody then ushers me to the door. It's the first time I have been to their house and not been offered any chocolate biscuits. I feel mildly disappointed, but then remember their doctor's appointment. Maybe it's to do with Mrs Peabody's knees. I turn to say goodbye and as I do, I notice some cat food in the porch. I didn't realise Mr and Mrs Peabody had a cat?

"Bye, Mrs Peabody," I call.

"Bye," and the door is shut even before she has finished saying the word. This robbery really does seem to have upset them.

I walk next door to Mr Snell. Now this is going to be tricky. He is not the most welcoming person as I have previously described, and I have only ever been into his house once when a package of ours was delivered to his house and I had to go to collect it. I stood in the hallway while he went to get the package from the living room and he then grunted at me when I said, "thank you."

I ring the bell and wait. I notice his head peer through the curtains as it often does, and eventually after what seems like ages, he answers the door.

"Yes?" Not very polite, don't you think?

"Um, Mr…Snell," I almost said Smell!

"Yes?" I'm surprised he can see me as he seems to be looking up not down!

"I wondered if you could help me, I'm doing a project on Australia and I know you have been there." I manage to get out.

"Yes?" Is this really the only word he knows?

"I thought I could maybe ask you a few questions?" I ask hopefully.

"Yes," This is really becoming quite dull now.

He stands aside which I take it means I can go in, so I step into his house and he leads me to the living room.

"Take a seat, I will be back in a minute," Oh, so he does know other words!

I sit down and look around. On the coffee table, I notice a mint wrapper. I quickly pull out my note book and start drawing.

What do you think? It looks like a match to the one I found at the side of Bluebird Bank. Hmm…

MINTS
MINTS

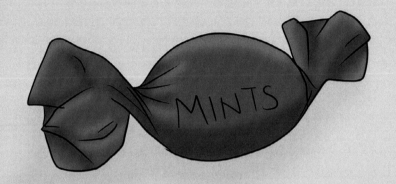

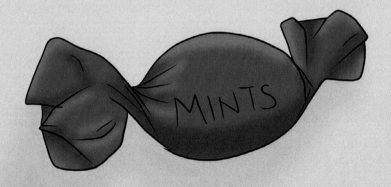

suspicious. I quickly use my tweezers to put the mint wrapper into one of my forensics bags and put it carefully into my rucksack.

It turns out Mr Snell knows a lot more words than I had initially thought. About one and a half hours of them to be precise. He showed me the photographs of his trip (all 1500 of them actually) and gave me lots of information although some of it was not so interesting (like the time he travelled to six different shops to find an Australian bush hat).

Anyway, it's been another successful day of investigating. I wonder if any of the fingerprints I have will match those found on the Armstrong's fence?

CHAPTER 8

Day 4 of the Investigation. Tuesday

"Mum, do we have to go today? I wanted to get on with some other stuff." Mum has arranged a trip to the library with Christopher and his mum followed by lunch back at our house. Izzy needs to borrow a book too, so she is coming with us.

"What other stuff, you are already halfway through your project on Australia and it is only Tuesday." I've actually finished it, I stayed up late last night using the book from Mr and Mrs Peabody (only after I had lifted their fingerprints off the book) and the information from Mr Snell.

"Well, I thought I might do some science experiments in my room." I could see already from Mum's expression what was coming.

"Hugo, you spend far too much time on your own doing science experiments which really only serves to damage your carpet even further. It's important you get out... and do other things. If you want, you can borrow a science book from the library and look at it with Christopher when you come home. We are leaving in ten minutes so make sure you are ready."

Oh well, fingerprint analysis will have to wait. I consider whether going to the library would help with the investigation in any way. Let's see, what do we know so far:

1. All the money in the bank's safe was taken.
2. It was taken at around 1.30 pm when the staff were having Mr Patel's cheese and tomato toasties for lunch.
3. The back door had been left open by Mrs Frank who was giving milk to a stray cat.
4. Mrs Armstrong's fence was damaged on the same day as the robbery.
5. The cat at number 22 was missing on the day of the robbery and turned up with an upset stomach and smelling very fresh the next day.
6. The bank was very clean when I inspected it.
7. The CCTV had been turned off.

I wonder how you can turn CCTV off? I wonder if you have to be actually in the building when turning it off, or whether there is a way you can do it from outside? That's it, I think, I am going to borrow a book about CCTV from the library. Instantly I feel cheered up. The day is not going to be wasted after all!

Mrs Harper has been the librarian at our local library for as long as I can remember. She is old, and when I say old, I mean really old. (And she looks it too!) She always wears brown, actually not really brown, more beige and this includes her socks which seem to gather at her ankles and her shoes. The entrance to the library is also beige and once she was standing against the door she was completely camouflaged. I got a complete shock when she said good morning. The thing about Mrs Harper is, she knows everything, and if she doesn't, she knows exactly where to find it. Behind her deceptive exterior she is a human computer. She really is amazing. Every time I see her it reminds me never to judge a book by its cover!

"How's your project on Australia going?" asks Christopher. He doesn't wait for a response.

"I haven't even started it, Mum says I should get some books out to help," he continues.

"It's going okay, why don't you look for the rough guide to Australia, I've heard it's a really good book," I reply. I would lend him Mr and Mrs Peabody's book, but they need it back by Friday morning for a quiz show they want to watch and besides I should ask them first before lending it out to other people.

"Okay, meet you back here in ten minutes," and off he runs.

Right, where would I look for a book on CCTV?

"Mrs Harper, I'm interested in how CCTV works and wondered if you could recommend any books?"

"Oh yes dear, look in the technology section aisle four number 200 – 336."

How does she remember all this?

"Oh, and Hugo, you might want to take a look at the magazines, especially Electronic Devices Today just in the box by the counter."

I walk over to the counter and see a box with about 15 copies of Electronic Devices Today. I'm sure I have seen this magazine before.

I flick through and see lots of articles about wiring, computers, tablets. Nothing of much interest here. Then something catches my eye. It's the most recent magazine. Only last month. The front cover story is 'the workings of CCTV page 14'. I can't believe it. I turn to page 14 and there it is, a four-page article on CCTV. The last page is all about how to turn off CCTV. From what I can understand, if the electrical box is outside of the building all you have to do is cut the black wire. This will completely disconnect the CCTV. The electrical box for the bank is outside the building and on Saturday morning the flap door to it was open.

Now, where have I seen this magazine before? I think back to the last few days. That's it. Mr Peabody was reading the same magazine when I went to their house to ask about Australia (but also to secretly get their fingerprints). Very curious.

That afternoon Christopher comes back to our house for lunch and then he, Izzy and I watch a movie. It's nice to have a break from the investigation and from worrying about Mum and Dad's money.

Before going to bed, I think about possible suspects.

1. Mrs Frank left the back door open, was that for a reason or by accident?
2. Mrs Armstrong's fence was damaged on the day of the robbery. Could she have climbed it to get to the bank?

3. Mr Snell had the same mint wrapper in his house that was found outside the bank. Could he have dropped it when robbing the bank?
4. Mr Peabody was reading a copy of Electronic Devices Today. Did he read about turning off the CCTV?

Who do you think it could be?

I think the only way to be sure is to check everyone's fingerprints.

CHAPTER 9

Day 5 of the Investigation. Wednesday.

I walk down the stairs to hear Mum and Dad's hushed voices. I stop to listen as any child would do in the same circumstances.

"What are we going to do? We had saved that money to take the children on holiday this summer," Mum says in a quiet whisper.

"We will just have to leave the holiday for this year and start saving again for next year," Dad replies calmly. "There is nothing we can do about it," he adds.

I turn around to see Izzy staring down the stairs too.

"It's not fair, Mum and Dad work so hard and they can't even have a holiday now because someone has stolen all their money, it's just not right," she says.

"Maybe the person will get caught?" I offer optimistically.

"No chance, they left no trace." She huffs and puffs down the stairs before I have the chance to respond.

I wouldn't exactly say they left no trace, would you?

After breakfast, I start my fingerprint analysis. I carefully place the fingerprints taken from the Armstrong's fence under one microscope and then under a second one I place the fingerprints I lifted off the Armstrong's remote control. I found four different fingerprints on the fence. Once I have eliminated the Armstrong family's fingerprints, the remaining ones will be the ones belonging to the people that delivered the fence and whoever is responsible for breaking the fence.

It's very tricky and you have to be very precise. Some of the fingerprints look identical except for one small detail. The key is to be slow and careful. (Accuracy is very important in science.)

After what seems like hours but actually only 15 minutes, I have eliminated two Armstrong fingerprints from the fence that matched fingerprints found on the remote control. Candy and Audi do not seem to have touched the fence.

Next, I place the remaining two fingerprints on the first microscope and Mr Snell's fingerprints on the next one. I really am hoping for a match (I always thought there was something very suspicious about him). Can you see the match?

No, unfortunately not.

There is a big difference right in the middle. I almost don't check Mrs Peabody's finger print. It seems a waste of time, but then I remember it is important to be thorough when undertaking any scientific investigation and I should really eliminate Mrs Peabody, just for the sake of completeness.

Next, I take Mr Peabody's fingerprint and immediately I see a huge difference between the two. I'm relieved and then tell myself of course there wouldn't be a match between the person who broke the Armstrong fence and Mr Peabody. He's a nice old man and 85.

I slide Mrs Peabody's fingerprint under the second microscope. I look closely. No, it can't be? I check again. There must be something wrong with my eyes. I check again. Definitely not, here take a look.

What do you think? It looks like a complete match.

I check for what feels like the 100th time and still they seem identical to me. It can't be? Why would Mrs Peabody's fingerprints be on Mrs Armstrong's fence?

CHAPTER 10

Day 6 of the Investigation. Thursday

I haven't slept all night. How could Mrs Peabody have anything to do with the robbery. It's absurd. There must be a logical explanation for why her fingerprint was on the Armstrong fence? But what? She never goes anywhere and the first time I saw her and Mr Peabody outside of their house was on the day of the robbery. It can't be her, can it?

I must look at all the evidence again.

I open my forensics kit and out falls the evidence bag containing some carpet fibres I had taken from the bank. Yes, I remember now, there was a very familiar smell on the carpet and some white dust, but I'm not sure what. That's it, I think. I know exactly what I'm going to do.

"Mum, would it be okay if I pop into the police station to ask how the investigation is going?" I ask.

Mum looks instantly alarmed.

"Why would you want to do that, Hugo? If they find something, they will let us know. The police station is not an appropriate place for children and we wouldn't want to get in their way," Mum replies.

"I promise I won't get in their way. I just want to ask if they have found anything and if you are worried about me, I could always ask Izzy to walk down there with me," I say in my most grown up and sensible voice.

Mum doesn't reply. I honestly don't think she knows what to say.

"I'm really interested in the investigation and think I may be more interested in detective work than science." Mum looks instantly relieved at the thought of me not being interested in science anymore. I think she thought it was an unhealthy obsession. I don't mention that the largest part of any crime investigation is the forensic science. She doesn't need to know that.

"Okay, okay," Mum says.

"But only if Izzy comes with you," she adds.

Izzy is busy 'texting' someone of great importance that she doesn't even look up when I go into her room or when I try speaking to her. I try for the third time to get a response from her.

"Could you please walk down to the police station with me, I just wanted to ask a few questions." On the third occasion, I finally get a response, although not the one I was hoping for.

"Why would you want to do that? It's so weird." She frowns at me.

"I'm just interested, please Izzy, Mum says I can't go unless you walk with me. I promise I will not say a word and you can carry on texting the whole time."

She grunts. This sounds hopeful. She gets up. Even more hopeful.

"Okay, but no more than ten minutes at the station, okay?"

"Yes, that's fine, thank you Izzy," I say eternally grateful.

We walk along Newport Street in silence. Izzy has the concentration of a surgeon performing open heart surgery when she is texting. Gosh, if she used that focus and concentration for other things, she could do something amazing. This is probably not the right time to raise this with her though.

We walk in through the grubby double doors to be greeted by Sergeant Lawlor. He is the shortest man I had ever seen who claims to be an adult (other than me of course). In fact, I can barely see his head over the counter. He had the roundest reddest face I have ever seen and if I squint my eyes, he really does look like a tomato. It doesn't help that he has no hair. If you close your eyes and imagine what you think a police officer would look like, it really wouldn't look like Sergeant Lawlor. His name is quite appropriate though, don't you think?

"Hello there, children, what can we do for you today?" he bellows. He doesn't look capable of speaking so loudly. Maybe it's part of the job description for all police officers to have such loud voices?

Izzy scowls and sits herself down on a chair and goes back to her phone. Meanwhile, Sergeant Lawlor is glaring at me and I can't help but to feel a little uncomfortable. Maybe this is one of his interrogation techniques. Stare and make people feel uncomfortable and they will confess all. Good tactic. I must remember this. I take a deep breath.

"I wondered if you had a forensic specialist here. I'm very interested in science and I wondered if I could ask a few questions."

Izzy looks up from her phone momentarily appalled and looks at me as if to say, "Is this the reason you have dragged me all the way here?"

I ignore her scowl.

"Well, as it happens there is someone, but she is very busy with the robbery and everything," he pauses, "but let me ask her, hold on here for a minute."

I wait almost holding my breath. Please, please, I recite over and over in my head.

Sergeant Lawlor returns smiling.

"Come on then," he calls raising the counter to let me in.

"Ten minutes!" shouts Izzy.

Sergeant Lawlor leads me into a white room at the end of a long dark corridor. A lady with what I can only describe as wild orange hair and the biggest smile I have ever seen stands up to greet me. She is wearing a white lab coat and is surrounded by the most amazing equipment I have ever seen. It looks like something out of a film.

"Hello, Hugo, my name is Sally Newton. I am the forensic investigator here. Sergeant Lawlor said you wanted to ask me some questions." She has an accent, but I'm not sure where from. Newton. Hmm…I wonder if she could be a distant relative of Sir Isaac Newton?

"Well, actually, I wondered if you would be able to test something for me." I am so in awe that my voice goes all squeaky. How embarrassing! I pull out the evidence bag from my back pack containing the carpet fibres from Bluebird Bank.

"These are some carpet fibres I pulled up from the carpet in the bank where the robbery took place last week. They smell slightly unusual and are covered in a white powder. I wonder if you could test them to see if you can identify the smell and what could be on the carpet," I say looking hopefully at her.

"Well, that is interesting. All the forensic tests I have done at the bank have come back with nothing unusual. However, testing the carpet fibres. That is very interesting and not something I would have thought about. Okay. I will do it and I will call you later this afternoon with the results," she says looking quite impressed.

"Thank you so much, Miss Newton," I reply, feeling a gush of pride. A real-life scientist (who incidentally may be related to Sir Isaac Newton) is actually impressed with me! I can't believe it!

Izzy and I walk home in silence and for the rest of the afternoon I skulk about waiting for the phone to ring.

Eventually at 4.05 pm the phone rings. Mum gets to it first.

"Hello, Baxter residence." This is Mum's standard statement whenever she answers the phone.

"Oh, yes Miss Newton, Hugo is here, I will just pass you over." Mum passes the phone across to me looking quite confused.

"Hello, Miss Newton," I say slightly nervously.

"Oh, hello, Hugo. I ran some tests on the carpet fibres you bought in. What I found was quite interesting." Miss Newton pauses.

"On testing, I found the following components. Sodium sulphate, calcium carbonate and a fragrance. Are you familiar with these substances, Hugo?"

"Well, as individual substances I have come across them in my experiments, but never together. I'm not sure what they would all be doing together," I say very confused.

"Well, this particular combination of chemicals is found in a particular cleaning product, better known as…Wave and Vax."

Surely not.

CHAPTER 11

Day 7 of the Investigation. Friday

Mr Peabody asked me to return the book about Australia by today so that is what I am going to do.

I am nervous, which before the start of this investigation was a feeling I had never really experienced before.

I ring the doorbell and wait. The door opens slowly. Mrs Peabody's head pokes out from a small gap.

"Can I help?" she says in a very abrupt way. Quite unlike Mrs Peabody.

"I've just come to return the book on Australia. Thank you so much, it was very helpful," I say trying to sound as normal and cheerful as I can.

Mrs Peabody opens the door a little wider so that she can take the book from me. As she does, I notice suitcases lined up in the hallway.

"Are you going somewhere?" I ask innocently. Mrs Peabody looks a little alarmed.

"Oh, yes, our Timothy has paid for us to go and visit him in Australia. We are leaving tomorrow at 12 pm," says Mrs Peabody rather too quickly.

Quick, I need to think fast. I need to get into the house to see what's going on.

"Would you mind if I use used your toilet? Izzy has been in the bathroom for the last two hours putting on her make-up, and I really am desperate," I say as politely as possible. Okay, so that was a slight exaggeration. Izzy has been in the bathroom for about 30 minutes.

"Um, well," Mrs Peabody hesitates.

"Um, well I suppose...O...o...o...okay." She stammers. She actually looks quite pale.

"But please be quick, we are very busy today," she adds as she reluctantly opens the door and the familiar smell of sodium sulphate, calcium carbonate and fragrance, aka Wave and Vax, hits me.

As I walk upstairs to the bathroom, I see Mr Peabody in the bedroom. He has his back to me and I can see he is franticly throwing clothes into a suitcase. His wardrobe doors are wide open, and I can see the wardrobe is completely empty. You don't take all your clothes when you are going on holiday?

I quietly close the bathroom door. It is the pinkest room I have ever seen. The tiles have pink splodges all over them and looks as though someone has eaten strawberry ice cream and then been sick all over the tiles. I am in a very bizarre situation of being inside Mr and Mrs Peabody's bathroom whilst they are packing all their clothes to go to Australia, and I'm not sure what to do.

I open the bathroom door slightly. Across the landing is the study. I creep out of the bathroom. Mr Peabody is still throwing clothes into a gigantic suitcase and I creep across to the study. It looks as though most things have been put into boxes. How long are they going for?

I see a notepad on the desk. I open the cover to see that the first sheet, although blank, has the indentation of a previously written note on top. I take out a pencil from my backpack and colour over the indentation to see if I can work out what was written on the previous note. I drop the pencil. This is what I see:

1. Climb over Armstrong fence.
2. Rob the bank at 1.30 pm.
3. Use Casper the cat to get the back door open.
4. Cut the CCTV wire from the electrical box at the back of the bank.
5. Take out all the money from the safe.
6. Hoover so there is no evidence left.
7. Use money to move to Australia.

"Is that you, Betty?!" I hear Mr Peabody shout. He must have heard the pencil drop. Wow, his hearing is impressive for an 85-year-old. I rip out the top sheet of the notepad and stuff it into my backpack and run down the stairs before Mr Peabody has the chance to turn around. I open the front door and run out and back home as fast as I can.

They have taken all our money. They are leaving tomorrow. I must stop them.

2 Rob The Bank
CCTV
money

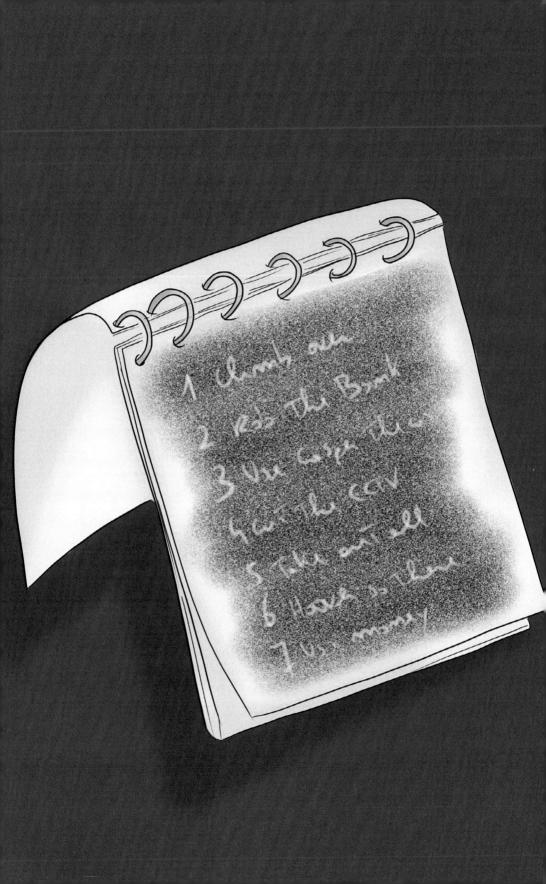

CHAPTER 12

Day 8 of the Investigation. Saturday 4 am

It's 4 am and Mr and Mrs Peabody are fast asleep. They will be leaving in eight hours to go to the airport with all our money. I must stop them leaving.

I take out all the science equipment I have as quietly as I can (Mum would not be happy with me waking her up at 4 am, she is already concerned about my unhealthy obsession with science). I need to somehow stop them from leaving in the safest way possible whilst I alert the police. (Safety is key to science.) I rack my brains. After speaking to Mum last night, it was clear she had no idea that the Peabodys were going away. She is planning to pop in on Sunday to check on them before we go to the science museum. So, they haven't told anyone they are going, so they probably want to leave quite quietly. That's it, I've got it! I will make sure they can't leave quietly.

I pull out my electrical kit and find what I'm looking for. It's a small bulb-shaped buzzer. I find my torch which has a pull switch and replace the bulb with the buzzer. I put the torch under my pillow to muffle the sound and pull the switch. Perfect. It makes a loud buzzing sound. I quickly turn it off.

So, this is my plan? What do you think?

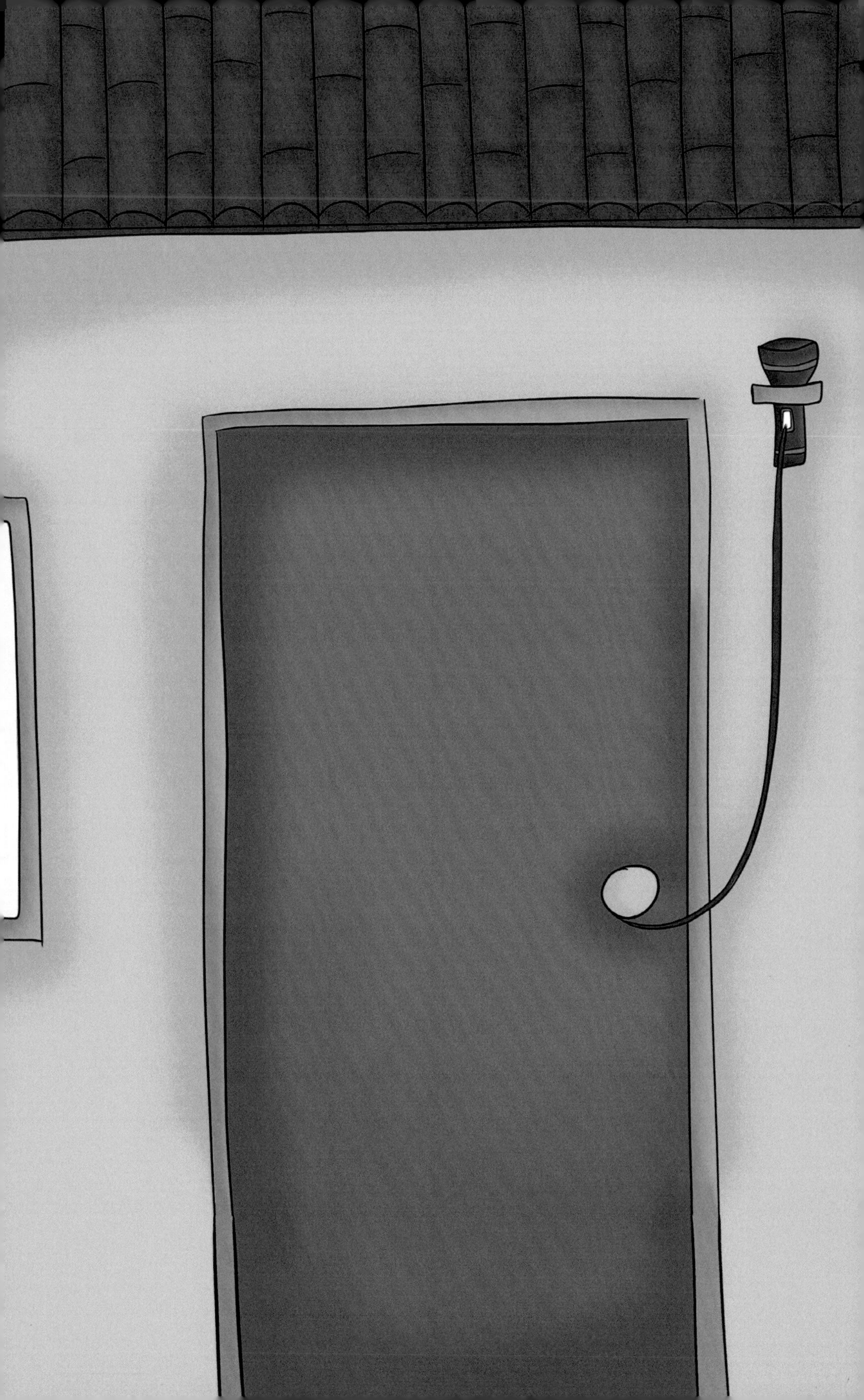

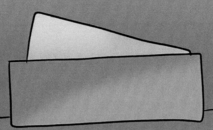

I am going to attach the buzzing torch to the outside of Mr and Mrs Peabody's house. I am going to attach one end of a strong piece of string to the pull switch and the other end to the door handle. When Mr and Mrs Peabody try to open the door, it will pull the string which will in turn pull the switch, making the buzzer go off. So, how does it work? For the buzzer to sound, there must be a flow of electricity from the battery to the buzzer and back again. There can't be any breaks in the flow. When the switch is off, there is a break in the flow, but the moment the switch is pulled, this creates a full circuit with no breaks and allows the electricity to flow. This leads to the buzzer sounding. I hope my diagrams of a closed and open circuit are useful.

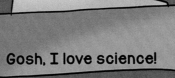

Gosh, I love science!

Now, time to get the plan into action. I creep downstairs and into the under stairs cupboard where the tool box is kept and find the duct tape and some very strong string. I put the door on the latch and creep next door. I realise very quickly that I am going to have to stick the torch quite high up on the bricks on the right-hand side of the door. I can't quite reach. I notice an empty plant pot and turn it upside down. I cut strips of duct tape and stick the corners to the side of the door. I then place the torch in exactly the right spot and carefully peel off the strips of duct tape and place them over the torch. My heart is really racing very fast. If Mum or Dad were to find out about this, I would be in big trouble. I then tie one end of the string to the pull switch on the torch and the other on the door handle. I must make sure the string is pulled as tight as possible between the torch and the door handle. There. All done. Now for part two of the plan.

CHAPTER 13

Still Day 8 on the Investigation. Saturday 10.30 am

Mum is in the shower and Dad is in the garden. I quickly slip out without them noticing. I won't be gone for very long. As I walk past number 98, I notice that my alarm is still alive.

At the police station, I am greeted by Sergeant Lawler with his tiny frame and huge voice.

"Hello again, Hugo, how can I help you today?"

"I have some information about the robbery at Bluebird Bank, I would like to talk to someone please?" I try to say in my most adult sounding voice.

Mr Lawlor is clearly amused and has a slight smirk on his face.
"Oh, really Hugo? I'm sorry to say that the big policemen are very very busy at the moment and it wouldn't be a good idea to waste their time. Perhaps you could ask your parents for some help. Now run along and play like a good boy."
Adults can really be so patronising!
"Sergeant Lawlor, I only need five minutes of your time, and you wouldn't want the suspects to get away?"
For a second Sergeant Lawlor looks concerned, but then a smile spreads across his face.

"Okay, okay, young Hugo, come on in, and I will get

Detective Singh for you."

I am led into a small room about the size of our bathroom. In the middle is a table with four chairs around it. The rest of the room is completely bare, with the exception of a huge clock on the wall. I am really starting to feel very uncomfortable. I sit down and go over my notes. A few minutes later Sergeant Lawlor and Detective Singh come into the room smiling at one another and sit opposite me. Detective Singh is absolutely huge in comparison to Sergeant Lawlor and I feel even more nervous now.

"Now, Hugo, you have some information for us," Detective Singh almost roars. I think it is definitely part of the job description to have a loud voice. Detective Singh looks over at Sergeant Lawlor again and smiles. They are humouring me, and that really annoys me. My nerves vanish instantly. I'll show them!

"Yes, I do." They smile at each other again. I carry on undeterred. How dare they!

"I visited the bank the day after it was robbed, and I took some samples of carpet fibres. There was a strong smell in the bank and the carpet was very clean. I was told that the back door had been left open as Mrs Franks had heard a cat at the back of the bank and opened the back door to give the cat some milk. Everyone knows that cats are lactose intolerant. I noticed that the back of the bank was parallel with all the houses on the same side of Newport Street. The first house was Mr and Mrs Armstrong's and I noticed that the fence was unsteady. On the way back, I noticed a sign to say that a cat was missing from number 22 Newport Street. I went to see the owner and was told that the cat had been missing the week of the robbery but had turned up on the day after the robbery with a very upset stomach and smelling very fresh. I then went to the Armstrong house and discovered that their new fence had been damaged on the day of the robbery. I took a sample of fingerprints from the fence. It looked like it had been climbed over. I went to Mrs and Mrs Peabody's house and noticed they had some cat food in their porch. They don't have a cat. I also noticed that Mr Peabody was reading a copy of Electronic Devices Today, which last month had an article about how to deactivate CCTV cameras. I tested the fingerprints from the Armstrong fence and found that there was a match between one of the fingerprints and Mrs Peabody's. I asked Miss Newton to test the carpet fibres for me and she found it contained Wave and Vax. Mrs Peabody is the only person I know to use Wave and Vax. I then went to Mr and Mrs Peabody's house and found this note in their study." I pass them the note and the fingerprint match and notice that both Sergeant Lawlor and Detective Singh have their mouths wide open and are completely motionless. I continue.

"Mr and Mrs Peabody are preparing to leave for Australia at 12 pm today. I have put together a make-shift alarm that will sound when they try to open the front door, so if they are hoping to leave quietly, they will be unable to, but we should get to them as quickly as possible."

At that moment, another police officer enters the room and turns to Detective Singh.

"Sir, we seem to have a problem at number 98 Newport Street, a resident called saying that a loud buzzer keeps sounding off," he says.

Sergeant Lawlor, Detective Singh and I all look at the clock on the wall. 12 pm. We scramble for the door.

"Quick, get the patrol cars and meet us at number 98 as fast as you can!" Detective Singh shouts out to the other police officer.

I race down the road behind the detective and sergeant, hoping that the Peabodys haven't escaped and that we are not too late.

As we approach number 98, we can see the Peabodys trying to open the door but the alarm going off every time. Great, we have made it in time.

"Hugo, go home, and we will be in to see you just as soon as we have spoken to the Peabodys," Detective Singh says in almost a whisper.

In the living room, Mum and Dad are peeking through the blinds. They turn to see me.

"Where have you been? What's going on next door? All we can hear is this loud buzzing noise and now the police are here?" Dad says in a flustered voice. He doesn't often get flustered.

I don't actually get the chance to respond.
"Oh, my goodness!" gasps Mum.

I look through the blinds to see Mr and Mrs Peabody being led away in handcuffs, a bottle of Wave and Vax hanging out of Mrs Peabody's cardigan pocket.

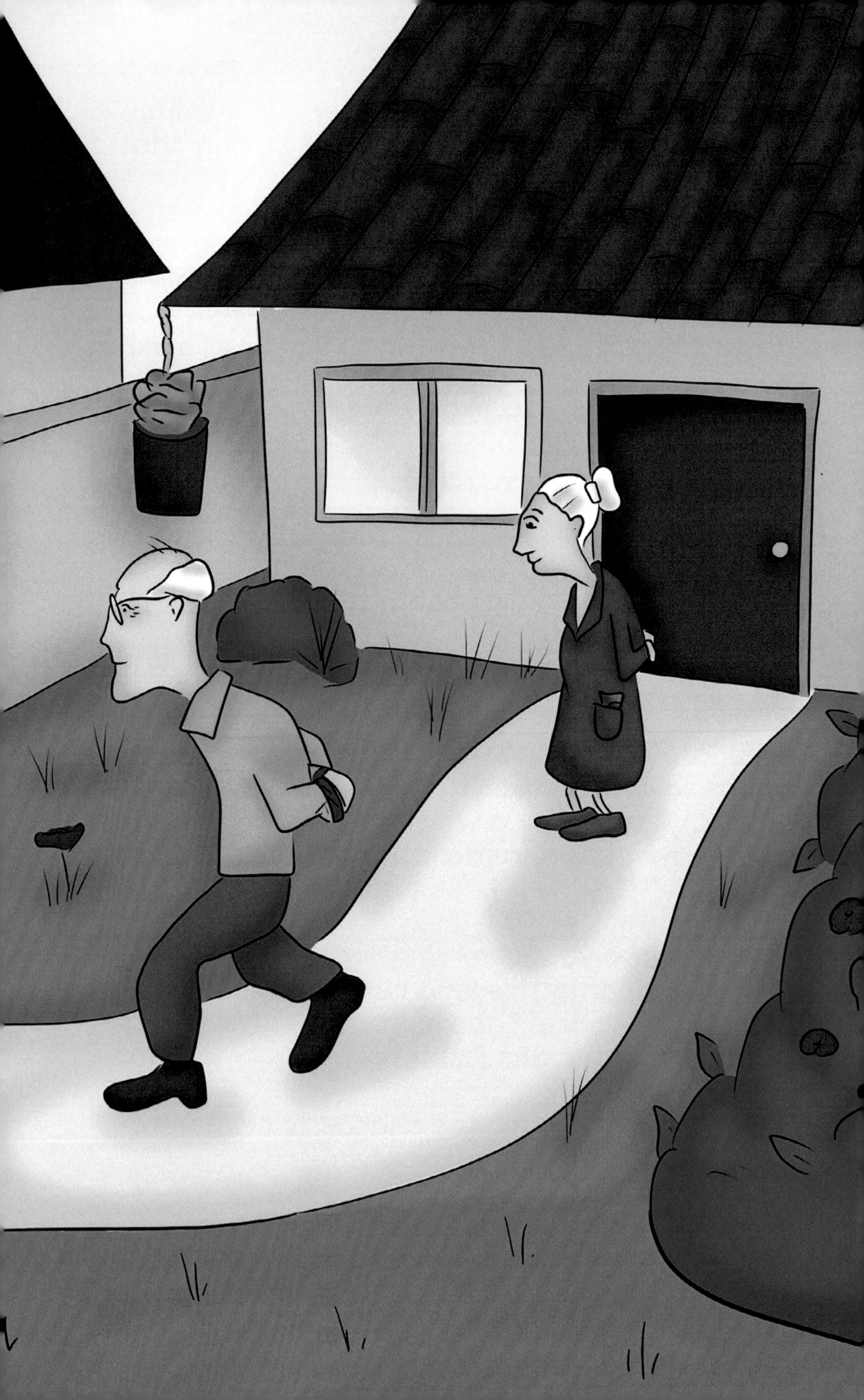

CHAPTER 14

8.20 am and the doorbell rings right on time. I open the door to see Christopher grinning. He hands me a copy of the Morning News which has a picture of me on the front cover. The headline is "Young Scientist saves the day". I must say, I am very pleased to be finally recognised as a scientist.

"I can't believe you solved the case, Hugo; you are brilliant, my parents are so pleased to have their money back and we are definitely going on holiday this year," he says.

After Mr and Mrs Peabody were arrested, Sergeant Lawlor and Detective Singh came to talk to my parents about what had happened. It turns out that Mr and Mrs Peabody had been planning the robbery for months. They had stolen Casper the cat in order to try and get the back door to the bank open. They had climbed over the Armstrong fence, but while climbing Mrs Peabody had an itchy nose so took off her glove to itch her nose, grabbed the fence to balance herself and accidentally left a fingerprint and nail marks on the fence. Mr Peabody cut the wire in the electrical box to deactivate the CCTV and had learnt how to do this from Electronic Devices Today, which he had subscribed to especially for the robbery. When they took the money from the safe, Mrs Peabody decided to hoover so that there was no trace and couldn't resist using her Wave and Vax which she apparently takes everywhere with her. The staff didn't hear the hoover as they were eating lunch behind the glass counter. Their plan was to leave the country and live in Australia with their son, Timothy. It also turns out that the mint wrapper I found outside the bank had Mrs Peabody's fingerprints on it. Apparently, Casper the cat's new fresh odour was down to the Wave and Vax. Detective Singh said that without my involvement, the Peabodys would never have been caught and my alarm stopped them from escaping.

My parents are very pleased. Mum said that she would never complain about my science experiments again. Dad says I am a brilliant scientist. Even Izzy was happy, and she even invited me into her room on Saturday evening so that I could tell her the whole story from start to finish. Turns out Izzy is actually really clever (I didn't notice before) and doesn't really like make up – she just wears it because everyone else does but has now decided to be more natural. She is fascinated by history with a particular interest in the Second World War. Not exactly science, but it was really nice getting to know her a bit better. She is definitely a lot friendlier towards me now.

Yesterday, we went to the science museum which was great as Mum didn't rush me, and I was allowed to spend hours in the electricity section looking at different circuits.

"Come on, slow coaches," Izzy calls back as she walks past. She is smiling. I notice she looks more like herself, not too much paint on today, which is nice. Number 98 is boarded up already. Mr Snell is standing in his doorway this morning. Most unusual.

He smiles, and it actually looks like a smile (he must have taken some lessons). I smile back.

At 102, the Armstrongs come out. Audi walks right in front of me and I try to move out of the way to avoid being knocked over and trampled on. Instead, the most surprising thing happens. Audi looks right at me, smiles and says, "Well done Hugo, for catching the robbers, I can get my new football now."

I really don't know what to say. I am not invisible!

Two very positive things emerged from having used amazing science to catch Mr and Mrs Peabody. The first is that I am now no longer invisible to the 'football group' or the 'computer game group'. The second is that Miss Little gave me an A+ for my project about Australia. I wouldn't have been able to do it without Mr Snell's information and, of course, Mr and Mrs Peabody's book on Australia.

The End

Why don't you have a go at drawing your route to school or a diagram of your house or school. You can take it to show your teacher at school.

GLOSSARY

Albert Einstein (1879–1955)
   Albert Einstein was born in Germany and had a great mind for maths and physics. From a young age he was interested in how things worked and was fascinated by a compass his dad gave him and why it was always pointing north. He became famous for his theory of relativity and his equation e=mc2 which shows that the tiniest things that are contained in everything can be turned into a huge amount of energy.

Alexander Graham Bell (1847–1922)
   Alexander Graham Bell grew up in Scotland and moved to Canada when he was 23. His mum and wife were both deaf and this influenced his work as he studied the human voice and experimented with sound. In 1876 he created the first working telephone. One of his famous quotes is "Before anything else preparation is the key to success."

Thomas Edison (1847–1931)
   Thomas Edison didn't do well at school and was home schooled by his mum. At the age of 12 he lost most of his hearing but considered this to be positive so that he could focus and concentrate more on his experiments and inventions. Thomas Edison would regularly spend 18 hours a day working and slept for only 4 hours! His greatest invention was lightbulbs for homes and the electrical system that powers them.

Marie Curie (1867–1934)

Marie who was originally born Maria in Poland had a strong interest in Physics. Marie worked as a teacher so she could save enough money to travel to France to study. Marie and her husband Pierre developed a theory of radioactivity which helped them to create a new treatment for cancer. She was the first woman to win a Nobel Prize and the first person to win two Nobel Prizes.

Stephen Hawking (1942 – 2018)

Stephen Hawking was raised in Oxford and went on to study at Oxford University. He studied science and then went on to study Maths and Physics at Cambridge University. At the age of 21 he was diagnosed with ALS, a motor neuron disease which resulted in him being wheelchair bound and he had to learn to communicate with a computerised voice. However, due to his determination, he continued to work and research in the areas of maths and physics and wrote many books. The most famous book is called A brief history in time and documents his research into how the universe began and how it continues to grow and expand.

Louis Pasteur (1822 – 1895)

French Scientist Louis Pasteur discovered his love of science when a teenager and went on to study science and maths at university and later became a chemistry professor at university. When his children became unwell Louis Pasteur focused his attention on investigating infectious diseases. He established that heating up liquids such as milk would kill bacteria making them safe to drink. This is known as pasteurisation and is still used today.

He was also instrumental in developing vaccines.

Sir Isaac Newton (1643 - 1727)

Sir Isaac Newton's family ran a farm in Woolsthorpe England; however, he was not interested in working on the farm and was more interested in his schoolwork. He studied at Cambridge University and later became a professor of Mathematics. He became famous for his work on discovering gravity and the laws of motion. Forces are measured in Newtons, named after Sir Isaac Newton!

The Periodic Table

The periodic table was invented by a Russian Scientist named Dmitri Mendeleev and contains all the known chemical elements that exist. There are 118 elements in the periodic table!